Scout & Lola ~ May all of your beary
Happiest of Dreams
come true

P.S. Please spit all
of your Pits B-4
you kiss your MAMA
B & FAT DADDIE Goodnight

Mani & Pitouee

THE TRUE LEGEND OF SLEEPING BEAR DUNES

Mani & Pitouee

THE TRUE LEGEND OF SLEEPING BEAR DUNES

Written by Paul H. Sutherland

Illustrated by Timothy M. Gibbons

道 KARUNA PRESS

道 KARUNA PRESS
111 Cass Street
Traverse City, MI 49684
pub@fimg.net

Sutherland, Paul H.

Mani & Pitouee: the true legend of Sleeping Bear Dunes / written by Paul H. Sutherland; illustrated by Timothy M. Gibbons. — Traverse City, MI: Karuna Press, 2005.

p.; cm.

Summary: A delightful tale about a little bear (Karuna), his otter friends (Mani & Pitouee), and how a playful cherry-spitting contest helped the Sleeping Bear Dunes and the Manitou Islands of northern Michigan get their names.
ISBN: 0-9661060-3-2

1. Sleeping Bear Dunes National Lakeshore (Mich.) — Juvenile fiction. 2. Sand dunes — Michigan — Juvenile fiction. 3. Otters — Juvenile fiction. 4. Bears — Juvenile fiction. 5. Legends — Michigan — Juvenile fiction. 6. Michigan — Juvenile fiction. I. Gibbons, Timothy M. II. Title. III. Mani and Pitouee.

PS3619.U844 M36 2005
813.6—dc22   0502

Printed in Canada

This book is dedicated to really old people and children

who pick up litter, clean their rooms, are kind to animals,

turn off the lights, brush their teeth, imagine, draw, paint,

dance in the woods, say their thank you and God Bless

prayers, share, tell stories, spit cherry pits, and yell

"can't get me!" as they swim and play.

—P.H.S.

To all those who do the right thing...you know who you are.

—T.M.G.

Timothy Gibbons

November 10, 2009

*E*ach year, on the longest day of summer, animals come from the north, south, east and west to the forest and sandy beach that is near Karuna Bear's house by what is now called Lake Michigan. The animal grownups come to talk about keeping the forests, lakes, streams and rivers clean and beautiful for all animals, insects, birds, and fish to enjoy.

This year they sat in circles and chatted about the land and how to help each other as they ate cherries, apricots, carrots, sweet corn, and maple candy.

It was time for Karuna Bear to go to bed.
Mother Bear tucked him in, "Tomorrow, Karuna,
animals from all directions will come to our woodland home to talk about what is old
and new! You must get a good night's sleep."

After tucking Karuna in bed, Mother Bear went downstairs to talk to papa and start planning. "I must make a list of good manners for Karuna to post first thing in the morning!"

But Karuna was not thinking about old or new; he was
thinking about spitting cherry pits. That night he dreamed he would
spit the farthest, beating the seven racoon siblings — who usually tied by
a few inches for the top seven spots in the kids' cherry-pit spitting contest.

Mother Bear asked her husband (who she called Fat Daddie because there was so much of him to love), "Did you tell all the animals to bring extra cherries this year?"

3 + 1 = 4

"Sure did, Lady-who-makes-my-heart-flutter-like-a-butterfly,"
replied Fat Daddie. This is what he called his wife. "The little critters will have plenty
of cherries to eat and spit! You and I will have plenty of time to sit back and listen to Old
Grampy Buffalo's stories and talk in the circle about keeping our land beautiful."

Animals, birds, and crawling creatures from all directions came

5 + 1 = 6

to the Bear's woodland near the Big Lake...

6 + 1 = 7

Mani and Pitouee, the otter twins, reached the woodlands first. They hurried up to Karuna who was busy pasting up signs with maple glue.

The otters were excited to tell Karuna about a new game called "Can't Get Me."

"The rules are simple," said Mani. "We'll swim around in the Big Lake while you all try to spit pits at us!"

Pitouee squeaked, "We'll dive deep in the clear water, pop up somewhere else and yell, "Can't Get Me! Can't Get Me!"

Karuna grinned at the otters, "Let's do it!"

The grownups gathered in their circles to talk about how they would keep their woodlands and waters clean while all the animal kids headed to the beach.

Karuna climbed a big cherry tree and yelled, "This year we're playing a new game called Can't Get Me!"

The animal children grabbed bowls and pails to hold their cherries. Parents filled them up with cherries from burlap sacks and bushel baskets.

Mani and Pitouee bounced out into Lake Michigan and shrieked, "Can't Get Me! Can't Get Me!"

The fox spit, the squirrel spit, even a worm spit a little pit! They spit pits everywhere!
Piles of cherry pits started growing along the lakeshore and woods.

The piles of pits started growing underwater too, but no one
noticed except an old crayfish whose front door was almost buried.

While the young animals laughed and played Can't Get Me, the parents were busy in circle meetings. They were very smart and knew it was important to talk about ways they can be kind, helpful and have good manners with each other and the land. They wrote all their ideas down.

Meanwhile, the animal kids were forgetting to bury their poop. The more cherries they ate, the more they pooped. Soon, it was getting stinky on the beach.

Whewwwweeeee!

Hold your pits kids~
This is one stinky
Beach !!!

Fat Daddie and Mother Bear came down to
the beach to see what all the commotion was about.
"Whewwwweeeee! Lady Bear who makes-my-heart-flutter-like-a-butterfly,
we have a stinky problem!" Fat Daddie pinched his nose.
Mother Bear smiled and said, "We must think of a solution! Who has an idea?!"

14 + 1 = 15

So every animal, bird, and crawling critter,
even the gnat on the horn of an elk, thought
of what they should do to clean up the messy beach…

15 + 1 = 16

Finally, a seagull named Gaia said,
"I know! What if a little one, like a mouse
or squirrel, climbed on my back and we
went to that sandy point that looks like
a pyramid and loaded up sand...."

"— and then brought it back here and dumped it
all over the pits and poop! Why, I could carry the racoon!"
said the Hawk. "And I will carry the Beaver," said the Eagle,
"Her tail will hold as much as a pail of sand!"

And that's exactly what they did. All the animals gathered sand and brought it back to dump on the piles of pits and poop. As they flew over Mani and Pitouee they dropped some of their sand, on them too. The otter twins kept yelling, "Can't get me!"

Soon, the mounds became great hills of sand. Two islands of sand rose out of the Big Lake.

Once all the sand was dropped,
    Karuna and the birds
        swept the sandy dunes
            smooth as a slide.

Mother Bear hugged Gaia, "Thank you for your lovely idea. Our land is so beautiful.
I can't wait for the stars and moon to look at our wonderful woodlands, islands and waters tonight."

20 + 1 = 21

Fat Daddie was pleased too. He announced, "It's getting late! Time for the bonfire. Kids, gather twigs and dry leaves. I'll find the biggest log in the forest to burn!"

That night the animals sang songs, ate cherry s'mores and told stories until everyone fell off into a deep slumber.

The next morning Mother Bear asked for everyone's attention. First she thanked the animals for being so kind and helping with the cleanup.

Then she said, "Before you pack up and leave I think we should name our sandy dunes and the two islands out there. Now, who has a name for them?"

The animals loved naming things! They all had a suggestion. The skunk yelled, "Stinky Dunes!"
The snake hissed, "Snake Pit Dunes," the pig snorted, "Piles of Pits Dunes!"
But they all agreed that the islands should be called the Mani and Pitouee Islands.

WE SHOULD CALL IT,
"SLEEPING BEAR DUNES"

Suddenly, Mani leaped into the air laughing,
"We should call it Sleeping Bear Dunes!"
and pointed at Karuna who was still sound asleep and snoring.

All the animals clapped and chanted, "Sleeping Bear Dunes, Sleeping Bear Dunes!" until Karuna opened a sleepy eye.

He yawned, "Waz goin on? Wha hapn'd?...I dreamed I was sleeping on a sand dune."

Fat Daddie and Mother Bear hugged Karuna,
"Yes, you were. You were sleeping on the Sleeping Bear Dunes!"

$26 + 1 = 27$

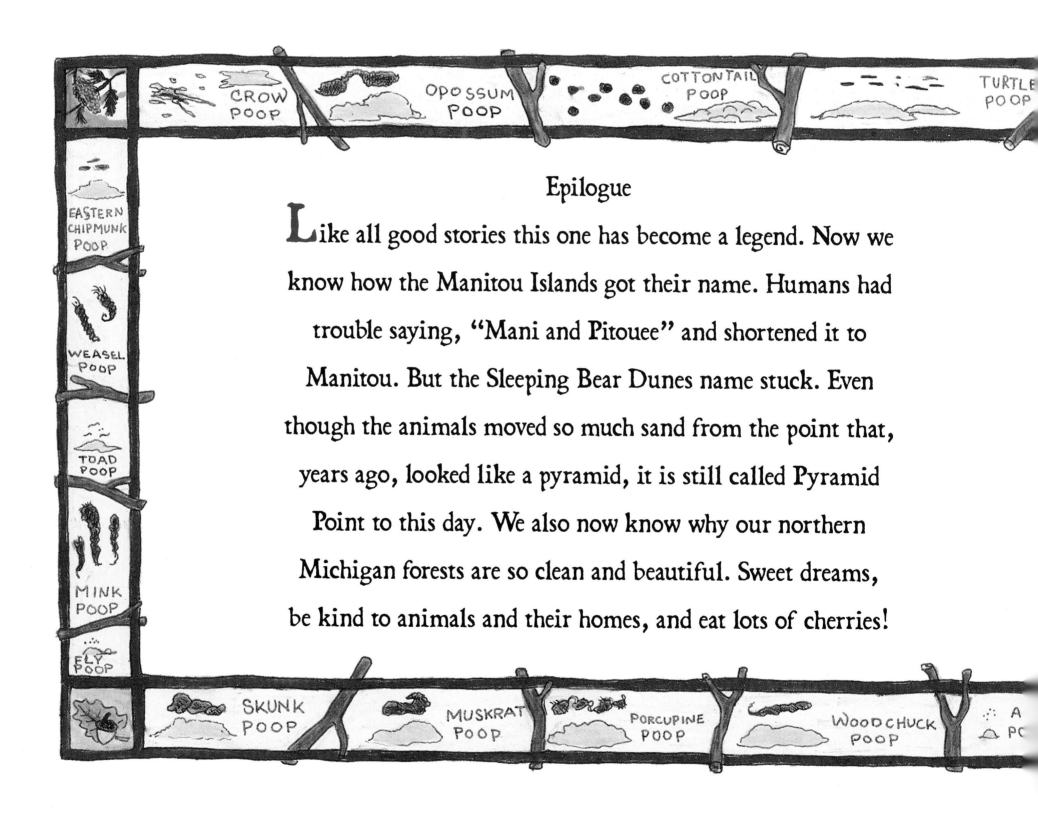

Epilogue

Like all good stories this one has become a legend. Now we know how the Manitou Islands got their name. Humans had trouble saying, "Mani and Pitouee" and shortened it to Manitou. But the Sleeping Bear Dunes name stuck. Even though the animals moved so much sand from the point that, years ago, looked like a pyramid, it is still called Pyramid Point to this day. We also now know why our northern Michigan forests are so clean and beautiful. Sweet dreams, be kind to animals and their homes, and eat lots of cherries!

A portion of the proceeds of *Mani & Pitouee: The True Legend of Sleeping Bear Dunes,* will go to some of our favorite endeavors, listed below:

Sleeping Bear Dunes National Lakeshore

Teaching Tolerance Project of the Southern Poverty Law Center

Great Lakes Children's Museum

Safe Passage / Camino Seguro

Michigan Land Use Institute

Interlochen Arts Academy / Pathfinder School

Animal Sanctuary

Helping Wildlife

Global Fund for Women

Share the World

Utopia Foundation

All the rest of the money is going to be spent on cherry pie, cherry ice cream, cherry gum, cherry gummi bears, fresh cherries, not-so-fresh cherries, sour cherries, cherry juice, chocolate-covered cherries, and family trips to climb the Sleeping Bear Dunes, walk the beach, go visit Mani and Pitouee on the Manitou Islands, and pens, pencils, and paints so we can create more books!

For years, Paul Sutherland has told his children, Keeston and Akasha, stories about mermaids, heroes, islands (lots of islands), otters, happy and helpful kids, exciting world adventures, and talking animals.

Paul, Keeston, and Akasha hope you enjoy *Mani & Pitouee: The True Legend of Sleeping Bear Dunes* and they would like to hear from you. The contact information is on the first page of this book.

They also hope that you will be kind to animals, the earth, and all people, including your brothers and sisters!

Timothy Gibbons was raised in northern Michigan where he loved running the dune beaches, collecting pockets full of rocks and driftwood for his grandfather who handcarved fish and birds.

For a few years, Tim and his wife migrated to New England's old salt air seacoast. They've recently flown home to nest with their young family along the shores of Lake Michigan.